To all the brave puppies
—E.B.

To Brandon, Jaimie, Claire, Reggie, Ed, Joyce,
my good friend Mr. Pickles,
and most of all to my wife, Debbie
—R.D.

Text copyright © 2013 by Eileen Brennan
Jacket art and interior illustrations copyright © 2013 by Regan Dunnick

All rights reserved. Published in the United States by Random House Children's Books,
a division of Random House, Inc., New York.
Random House and the colophon are registered trademarks of Random House, Inc.

Visit us on the Web! randomhouse.com/kids
Educators and librarians, for a variety of teaching tools, visit us at RHTeachersLibrarians.com

Library of Congress Cataloging-in-Publication Data
Brennan, Eileen.
Bad Astrid / Eileen Brennan ; illustrated by Regan Dunnick. — 1st ed.
p. cm.
Summary: Bad Astrid has been terrorizing everyone and everything on her block ever since her family moved in.
But when an accident befalls the bully, it's up to a new neighbor to teach Astrid how to be a friend.
ISBN 978-0-375-85580-1 (trade) — ISBN 978-0-375-95580-8 (lib. bdg.)
[1. Stories in rhyme. 2. Bullies—Fiction.] I. Dunnick, Regan, ill. II. Title.
PZ8.3.B7447Bad 2013 [E]—dc23 2012019018

MANUFACTURED IN CHINA
10 9 8 7 6 5 4 3 2 1
First Edition

BAD ASTRID

story by
EiLEEN BRENNAN | **ReGaN DUNNiCK**

pictures by

Random House 🏠 New York

She came into town
like five tons of **bad** luck.
She came into town
in a **big** moving truck.

MeaNer than any girl
you'll ever meet—

and she and her family
moved in down the street!

Astrid was at least
four feet two,
WITHOUT SOCKS!

She was boxy and solid,
like a **cabinet** that
talks.

A cranky, crabby troll,
Astrid barked and stood guard.
She'd **gROWL**, **Spit,** and **Sputter**
if I walked past her yard.

She chased little chipmunks,
pOppEd heads off of flowers.

She spent her time **teasing** my poor bird for hours.

She loved to **destroy**
any fun I had planned.
    She'd squirt-gun chalk drawings,
    topple my lemonade stand.

In her bike helmet painted
with a skull and crossbones,

she **tore up** the sidewalk
like a mini-cyclone.

And she would

never,

ever,

ever

leave me alone!

Such a **Nasty** new neighbor—
yes, it was quite a bummer.

But I would *not* allow her
to ruin my summer. . . .

I'd learn knitting,

the tango,

and new karate kicks,

and build a small Eiffel Tower
out of Popsicle sticks!

So I danced, kicked, and built,
knit a seven-foot-long cap!

Then one day the ground **rUMbLed**,
and I heard branches snap.

Through our hedge she came **CRaSHiNG**,
but she didn't come alone—

she brought a stop sign, our mailbox,
and our neighbor's lawn gnome.

But still her bike rolled,
and my heart sank a trifle

as there came crashing down
my Popsicle stick Eiffel!

Astrid lay tangled
like a set of jumbled keys.
As I slowly crept close, I heard,

I felt sad. I felt angry.
I was just about to cry,
but I stiffened my lip bravely,
and instead I asked, **"Why?"**

"**Why** are you mean to me?
And look at this mess!"

Astrid stuttered,
"I . . . I'm *sorry*. . . .
I just wanted attention, I guess."

I began counting all the damage
but realized before the end
that my abominable new neighbor
could really use a friend.

So I pulled her from the wreckage,
got a bandage for her knee.
Astrid gathered Popsicle sticks
and handed them to me.

Then Astrid surprised me—
she hugged me like a vise!

I realized, yes, Astrid's bad,

but she can also be

quite

Nice!